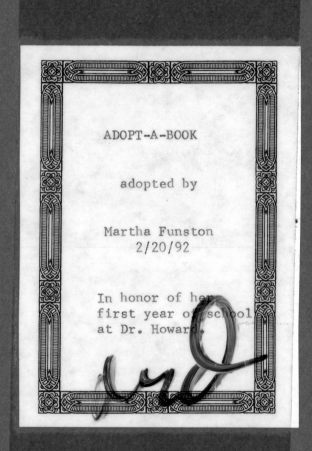

ADOPT-A-BOOK

adopted by

Martha Funston
2/20/92

In honor of her
first year of school
at Dr. Howard.

HOT FUDGE

HAROLD & CHESTER

I N

HOT FUDGE

JAMES HOWE

Illustrated by

LESLIE MORRILL

Morrow Junior Books / New York

To

MARILYN & NEIL, RACHEL & SHIRA—

and chocolate-lovers everywhere

Text copyright © 1990 by James Howe
Illustrations copyright © 1990 by Leslie Morrill
All rights reserved.
No part of this book may be reproduced or utilized
in any form or by any means, electronic or mechanical,
including photocopying, recording or by any information
storage and retrieval system,
without permission in writing from the Publisher.
Inquiries should be addressed to
William Morrow and Company, Inc.,
105 Madison Avenue,
New York, NY 10016.
Printed in the United States of America.
1 2 3 4 5 6 7 8 9 10
Library of Congress Cataloging-in-Publication Data
Howe, James, 1946–
Hot Fudge / James Howe ; illustrated by Leslie Morrill.
p.   cm.
Summary: The Monroe family tests Harold the dog's willpower when
they leave him alone with a pan of fudge.
ISBN 0-688-08237-8. — ISBN 0-688-09701-4 (lib. bdg.)
[1. Fudge—Fiction.   2. Chocolate—Fiction.   3. Dogs—Fiction.   4. Cats—Fiction.]
I. Morrill, Leslie H., ill.   II. Title.   III. Title: Hot Fudge.
PZ7.H83727Har 1990
[E]—dc20   89-13468   CIP   AC

A Note to the Reader

The story you are about to read is told by a dog. But Harold is no ordinary dog. He has written other books about his family, the Monroes, and about his friends—Chester, a cat; Howie, a dachshund puppy; and Bunnicula, a most unusual rabbit.

When Harold sent this story to me, he enclosed a note that read:

It is no secret that I love chocolate. So does Toby, one of the Monroes' two sons. One day Toby had a surprise for me, and I just knew it had something to do with our favorite food. What I didn't know was that Toby's surprise wasn't the only one that the day held in store.

I admit my mouth was watering as I sat down to read Harold's latest adventure. Luckily, I always keep a little something to munch on while I read. You might want to, too. But if what you're munching on is fudge, keep your eye on it. It just might disappear!

—THE EDITOR

Friday nights are special at our house. Toby gets to stay up and read as late as he wants. He lets me lie on his bed with him and share his chocolate treats. Toby and I love chocolate. I lick his fingers all over so he won't get sticky, brown smudges on the pages of his books.

They frown on sticky, brown smudges down at the library.

When Toby gets tired, he brushes his teeth, turns out the light, and says, "Good night, Harold. Sweet dreams." And then we fall asleep, full of good stories and good chocolate.

One Friday night, Toby whispered in the dark, "Wait until tomorrow, Harold. Yum, yum. Just wait."

If I didn't love sleeping almost as much as eating, I would never have slept that night. *Yum, yum. Just wait.* What did Toby mean?

When I woke the next morning, my nose figured out the
answer even before my brain remembered the question.

FUDGE. Mr. Monroe was making his famous fudge!

"Chester!" I cried, as I skidded across the kitchen floor. Chester looked up calmly from his food dish. "How can you eat that *stuff* when there's fudge in the air?" I asked.

"Because," said Chester, "the fudge is in the air and not in my bowl. And I'm hungry."

He had a point.

After wolfing down my breakfast, I joined Howie to beg at Mr. Monroe's side.

"Have you no shame?" Chester asked. He says that sort of thing whenever Howie and I beg and whimper.

"We're dogs," I told him. "Begging is one of the things dogs do best. Besides, don't tell me there's anything more dignified about rubbing up against people's legs and leaving little hairs all over their pants."

Chester stuck his nose in the air and walked away. I turned my attention back to more important matters.

"Nice try, fellas," Mr. Monroe said as we whimpered. "But this fudge isn't for you."

Not for us? But Toby said—

Just then, the kitchen door flew open and the rest of the Monroe family rushed in.

"That fudge sure smells good!" Toby cried. "Can I lick the spoon?"

"*After* breakfast," said Mrs. Monroe. "*If* there's time. I just discovered the station wagon has a flat tire. We'll have to use one car."

"But I've got to get to practice *now*," Pete whined.

"Dear," Mrs. Monroe said to her husband, "I'll drop you and Toby off first, then Pete and I will go on to the field. All right?" Mrs. Monroe was Pete's weekend soccer coach.

"Fine, fine," said Mr. Monroe. "I just need a little more time for this second batch of fudge to cool."

"But *Mom*," Pete whined again.

"Ten minutes?" Mrs. Monroe asked.

Mr. Monroe nodded.

"Ten minutes," said Mrs. Monroe.

Everybody started running in and out of the kitchen and
up and down the stairs, shouting and banging things and
slamming doors.

It was a typical Saturday morning.

And then:

"Goodbye, Harold!"

"Goodbye, Chester!"

"Goodbye, Howie!"

"Goodbye, Bunnicula!"

The doors stopped banging. The house grew quiet. And Howie and I suddenly found ourselves alone in the kitchen.

Alone with a plate of fudge.

"This isn't fair, Uncle Harold," Howie complained. "Do you think they're testing us?"

Oh, that smell! It was enough to make your taste buds weep.
"Yes," I said. "And we're about to flunk. Let's get out
of here."

Chester had wandered off to the living room, where we found
him reading the newspaper in his favorite chair.

"Anything interesting in the fudge?" I asked. I'd meant to say
"paper."

"Harold," Chester said, "you have chocolate on the brain. You
can't spend the day like this."

"I have an idea," said Howie. "Let's play a game. How about Rip-the-Rag? Or Bury-the-Bone?"

"Yipes!" Chester exclaimed.

"I don't know that one," I said. "How do you play it?"

"It isn't a game," Chester said. "I just read in the paper that there have been a number of robberies recently. During the day. *In this neighborhood!*

"We're going to have to guard the house, Harold. That's what pets are for. I know, I know—you're going to say pets are for loving and snuggling and rolling around with on the floor, but let's face it. We're really just a cheap burglar alarm system."

"I'd rather snuggle," I muttered, as Howie began to yip. But I knew it was useless to argue with Chester. Once he has made up his mind about something, that's the end of it.

So Howie guarded the front door.

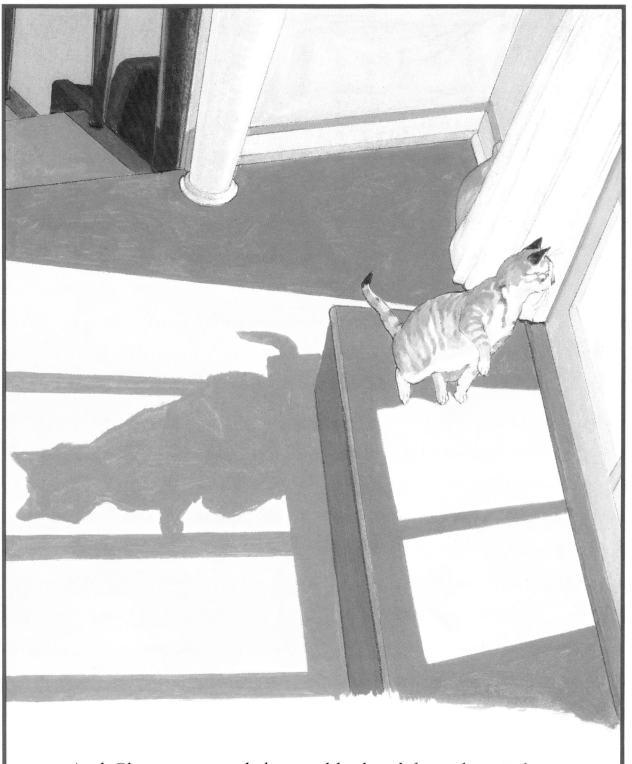

And Chester surveyed the neighborhood from the window at the top of the stairs.

And I positioned myself at the kitchen door.
Near the fudge.

Now I don't know how long it's been since you've protected your house against robbers, but if it's been a while, let me remind you that it isn't all it's cracked up to be. The truth is that it gets boring. Fast! It wasn't long before I was sound asleep.

I was having the most wonderful dream when a loud BANG
woke me.

"Chester!" I cried.

Chester raced into the kitchen. "I heard it, I heard it!" he
said.

Howie straggled in. "Heard what?" he asked, with a yawn. I couldn't help myself. I yawned, too.

"Don't tell me you two have been sleeping," Chester said.

"Okay, we won't tell you," said Howie.

Chester shook his head. "They should call them dognaps, not catnaps," he said. "Don't you realize what's happened? There's been a robbery. Look, the pan of fudge is missing from the counter!"

"Missing?" I said.

"Stolen!" said Chester.

"Stolen?" Howie cried in amazement. "You mean it's *hot fudge?!*"

"The thief can't be far away," Chester said. "Come on, you two. Put those doggie sniffers to use!"

We were almost out the pet door when I looked up and spotted a pan sitting on the windowsill.

"Wait," I said. "The fudge hasn't been stolen; it's just been moved."

"Who would move it?" Chester asked. He gave me a funny look. "Harold," he said, "shame on you!"

"I didn't touch it! I was *dreaming* about it, I admit, but—"

"*You* can reach it, Uncle Harold," said Howie. "See if it's been touched."

I put my front paws on the sill, raised myself up to my full height, and peered over the top of the pan. I could hardly believe my eyes!

"It's turned white!" I said.

"*White?*" Chester gasped. "Well, I guess we know who the culprit is, don't we?"

And he dashed through the door into the living room.

Howie and I followed after him.

Bunnicula was sleeping soundly in his cage.

"Don't be fooled," Chester whispered. "He's pretending to be asleep."

Chester believes that our little bunny is a vampire. Up until now, Bunnicula had only sucked the juices out of vegetables, turning them white. But as Chester pointed out, there was no reason he might not turn fudge white as well.

"Maybe he has a sweet fang," he suggested.

"What's wrong with that?" Howie said. "At least the fudge wasn't stolen."

"But what about that *bang* we heard?" I asked.

Before anyone could answer, another loud BANG sounded from the kitchen.

This time, the fudge was gone! *Really* gone!

The three of us pushed and shoved our way out the pet door.
No sooner were we outside than we spotted the thief in the
distance, running away.

"Stop! Thief!" Chester shouted.

Howie barked excitedly. "He's got the fudge! What kind of lowlife would steal *candy?*" He yipped out warnings to the neighborhood: "Guard your gumdrops! Lock up your licorice!"

We were closing in on him. We had him. The chocolate thief
had fallen. We had captured…

Toby!

"What's the matter with you guys?" he said, getting up. "Are you nuts?"

He noticed the way I was staring and started to laugh. "Just nuts about fudge, huh, Harold? Couldn't let it out of your sight, could you? Well, if you think Dad's fudge is something, just follow me."

I could hardly believe my eyes: this was the nearest thing to heaven I'd ever seen!

"We were in such a rush to leave this morning, we forgot to take the two pans of fudge Dad made," Toby explained. "Then when I ran home to get them, I forgot about the one made with white chocolate because it was up on the windowsill. I was all the way down the block before I remembered and had to turn back."

Toby gave me a little taste of the white fudge. It was okay. But if you want my expert opinion, if it isn't brown, it isn't chocolate.

"Gee," Toby went on, "to think you were in the house all that time with all that chocolate and you never even *touched* it. That deserves a reward!"

"Make mine catnip," Chester said.

Each to his own taste. But I knew what Toby had in mind.

Sweet dreams!

Mr. Monroe's Famous Fudge

If you and a grown-up would like to make Mr. Monroe's famous fudge together, here's the recipe. *Do not use the stove or handle sharp knives by yourself!* This fudge will taste good whether it's made by two hands or four. And don't forget to let "hot fudge" get cool before eating it.

Ingredients:
2 ounces of unsweetened chocolate, in squares or liquid packets
1/3 cup of light corn syrup
1/2 cup of milk
2 cups of sugar
2 tablespoons of butter
1 teaspoon of vanilla
chopped walnuts to taste

Put the chocolate, corn syrup, milk, and sugar in a deep saucepan and cook over *low* heat. Stir constantly until everything is dissolved completely. Turn the heat up slightly and boil slowly until the chocolate forms a soft ball in cold water. (This part can be tricky. Drop a little bit of the chocolate into a cup of cold water with a spoon, wait a few seconds, then try to form the chocolate into a soft, slightly squishy ball that rolls gently between your fingers. If it falls apart, it's too liquidy, so boil it a little longer. You may need to repeat this test frequently until the chocolate is the right consistency.) Remove the saucepan from the heat. Stir in the butter and vanilla. Let the mixture cool for ten to fifteen minutes. Then beat it with a large spoon, a strong arm, and patience. Beating, by the way, isn't the same as stirring; beating means to stir *vigorously*, like you mean it! Better yet, why not hand the pan over to the grown-up who is cooking with you. The fudge has been beaten long enough when you can feel it thickening and the surface loses some of its shine and begins to look a little dull.

Stir in the nuts. Pour the fudge into a lightly greased pie plate or pan. Let the mixture sit until it's cooled completely. Have the grown-up cut the fudge into pieces with a sharp, moist knife. Pour yourselves some milk and dig in.

NOTE
Harold is an unusual dog in many ways. He reads, he writes, and he loves chocolate. But chocolate is not a good food for most dogs; in fact, it makes them sick. Share your fudge with people only. And give your dog another kind of treat—one that's just right for him or her.

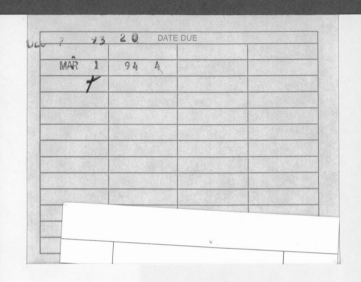

E
HOW

Howe, James.
Harold & Chester in
hot fudge.